You go to school every day.

So does Patrick.

Maybe you ride on a schoolbus.

So does Patrick.

After school you play with your friends.

So does Patrick.

In fact, there's only one difference between you and Patrick.

But it is a *big* difference.

Patrick is a dinosaur. A *big* dinosaur.

Patrick's friends are dinosaurs, too.

So is his teacher.

So are his Mom and Dad.

What's it like to be a student in a school for dinosaurs?

That's what Dino School is all about!

Dino School

SNEEZE-O-SAURUS

Jacqueline A. Ball
Illustrated by David Schulz

A TRUMPET CLUB SPECIAL EDITION

Dedicated to my brother, Joseph Gary Ausanka, my dear sister-in-law Liz, and my favorite niece and nephew, Kristen and Justin.

Published by The Trumpet Club
666 Fifth Avenue, New York, New York 10103

Copyright © 1990 by Jacqueline A. Ball

ISBN 0-440-84837-7

This edition published by arrangement with
HarperCollins Publishers
Cover and interior design by Nancy Norton, Norton
& Company
Printed in the United States of America
November 1991

10 9 8 7 6 5 4 3 2 1
OPM

CHAPTER
1

The cold December wind blew against the windows at Dino School.

The windows shook and rattled.

Snow piled up in the corners.

But inside Room 211 it was warm and cozy.

The teacher in Room 211 was named Mrs. Diplodocus. Her students called her Mrs. D.

Mrs. D.'s room was decorated for Christmas and Hanukkah.

There were red and green paper chains on the bulletin boards.

There were red bows on the plants and on the fish tank.

There was a golden Hanukkah menorah on a table.

Even Mrs. D. was decorated. She wore four necklaces around her long, greenish-blue neck. The necklaces looked like strings of snowflakes.

Sara Triceratops thought Mrs. D.'s necklaces were pretty. She loved snow. Especially at Christmas.

Sara watched the snow drift against the windows. *Only one more week until Christmas,* she thought. *I can't wait!*

Mrs. D. was reading a story to the class. It was one of Sara's favorites: *Frosty the Snow Dino.*

"And then Frosty began to dance," she read.

Someone started to sniffle.

Sniff. Sniff.

Mrs. D. kept reading. "Then Frosty began to sing."

There were more sniffles.

Sniff sniff. Sniff sniff.

2

"Then Frosty ran over the hill and waved and said—"

AH-CHOO!

Mrs. D. put down the book. "Patrick, was that you?"

Patrick Apatosaurus was holding his handkerchief. It was the size of a bedsheet.

Patrick was the biggest dino in Mrs. D.'s class.

He blew his nose. HONK!

"I don't feel well," he croaked.

"Poor thing!" said his teacher. "You sound terrible!"

AH-CHOO! AH-CHOO!

Sniffle. Sniffle.

Cough cough cough cough COUGH!

The whole room seemed to explode in one dino-sized cold.

"My throat hurts," complained Sara's very best friend, Annette Anatosaurus.

"My head hurts," complained Hank Ankylosaur.

"My horns hurt," complained Sara's twin brother, Ty.

"Baby," she hissed. "Big baby."

Ty didn't even make a face at her. Or tell her to take it back.

He must be sick, Sara thought.

Patrick sneezed again.

The sneeze blew off the baseball cap he always wore.

It blew Sara's notebook off her desk.

"Sorry," Patrick croaked. He looked as sick as he sounded. His eyes were watery and red.

"That's okay," Sara said. She picked up her notebook and Patrick's Denver Dinos cap.

She held the cap by her fingertips. She didn't really want to touch it.

She liked Patrick a lot. In fact, she

had a giant crush on him. But she didn't like his germs. She didn't want them on her. It would be awful to be sick for Christmas.

"Here," she said, smiling.

Patrick took the cap as the bell rang.

Usually the dinos stampeded out of the room. Today they walked slowly. Heads and tails drooped.

"Now, stay home tomorrow if you're sick!" Mrs. D. called after them. "Let's all be well for our trip to Cave City on Friday."

The whole class was excited about going to Cave City. Every year there was a school Christmas party at the big outdoor skating rink there.

The best part of it was a Christmas ice show with Tory Pterodactyl and the Ice Screams. They were ice skaters who did fancy tricks in Christmas costumes.

Sara had seen them on TV. They were fantastic. She couldn't wait to see them live at Cave City.

Sara stopped at her locker. She pulled on her bright yellow boots. She tied her warm yellow scarf around her neck. Then she caught up with Annette and Spike Stegosaurus.

"You look awful," Sara told Annette.

Annette's nose was red and shiny.

"Sort of like Rudolph the Red-Nosed Rein-Dino," agreed Spike.

Spike was the coolest dino in school. He wore supercool sunglasses and clothes that were a special brand. Dino-Dude Duds.

He'll never get sick, Sara thought. *He's too cool.*

Annette didn't smile. "Go ahead, make fun," she said. "Just because *you* two aren't sick."

"Yet," added Ty from behind.

7

Sara turned her head.

Ty coughed in her face.

She leaped back. "Ugh! Gross! Cut it out, Ty! Keep your disgusting germs to yourself!"

Up ahead, Patrick was blowing his nose again.

HONK! HONK!

Sara couldn't wait to get home. At least she'd only have Ty's germs to worry about there.

She hurried out of school.

She waded through knee-deep snow to her bus.

The air was cold on her face. She felt snowflakes landing on her horns.

Then something smashed against the back of her neck. It was soft and cold. Icy trickles ran down her back. They made her shiver.

She reached back and pulled a handful of snow out of her collar.

8

"Ha, ha," a gruff voice yelled.

Sara whirled around.

Another snowball hit her on her middle horn. Snow sprayed out into a white cloud.

The voice laughed again. "Can't ya catch?"

Sara wiped her eyes. She saw a big, mean-looking dino near the bike rack. He wore a black ski jacket and black boots.

It was Tyrannosaurus Rex.

Rex was the biggest bully in Mrs. D.'s class.

He was the biggest bully in the whole school.

Maybe in the whole town.

"Rex," Sara shouted. "Stop it!"

Another snowball hit her nose.

"Oo-ee! Bull's-eye!"

"Ouch! Annette! Ty! Spike!"

There was no answer.

Probably already on the bus, she thought angrily. *Thanks a lot, guys.*

She wiped her eyes again.

Now she could see more snowballs flying through the air. Dozens of them.

She ducked and ran.

But the snowballs were headed *away* from her. Toward Rex!

One hit him in the right shoulder.

"Strike one!" a voice called.

One hit him in the left shoulder.

"Strike two!"

One hit him in his mouth full of jagged teeth.

"Strike three, and Rex is O-U-T!"

It was Spike. He was behind a bush. Snowballs were piled beside him. He was batting them at Rex with his tail.

"You're dead meat, Stegosaurus," Rex shouted.

"Run for it!" Spike called to Sara.

Splat! Two big snowballs knocked

Rex's bike over into the snow.

"Strike four!" voices yelled from Sara's bus. "Your bike's out, too!"

Annette and Ty were leaning out the window.

Sara leaped on the bus and sat down behind them. She was panting.

From the window she could see Rex leaning over his bike. He looked furious.

Sara shuddered. Rex hated it when anything happened to his bike. He might be mad enough to do something *really* mean.

She tapped her brother on the shoulder. "Thanks," she said.

"Annette smuggled the snowballs on the bus," said Ty. "And I threw them."

Annette smiled proudly. Then her face twisted up.

"AH-CHOO!"

CHAPTER
2

Coughs and sneezes filled the air on the bus. Sara scrunched down into a corner of the seat. She wrapped her scarf tightly around her mouth and nose so no germs could leak in.

Germs, germs, go away, she sang to herself. *And don't come back on Christmas day!*

When the bus reached her stop, she leaped off.

Ty followed slowly. His tail dragged through the snow.

Mrs. Triceratops was in the kitchen. She was still wearing her coat.

Little Tracy Triceratops sat in her high chair. She squirmed as her mother pulled off her boots.

"Hi, Mom," said Sara.

She patted her little sister's head.

"Fumpf," fussed Tracy. She was only one year old.

"Hi, dear," said her mother. "We just got home from the sitter's."

Sara grabbed some apples from the bowl. She rubbed them on her scarf.

She liked her apples shiny.

She opened her mouth to take a bite. Then she noticed something.

Tracy's nose was red. Her eyes were watery.

"Tracy doesn't feel well," her mother said.

Germs! Sara thought. On her hand, where she had patted Tracy.

Quickly she went to the sink and scrubbed her hands.

Ty shuffled into the kitchen. "I don't feel well, either. My horns ache. I can't lift my tail."

"Oh, Ty! You look terrible!" his mother exclaimed.

"Even worse than usual," Sara agreed.

Ty scowled at her. His face was a sick pink color. Usually he looked green and healthy.

"There's a flu bug going around," Mrs. Triceratops said. "It only lasts a day or two, but it can be pretty awful. Better get up to bed, Ty."

Sara plunked herself down on a stool. It was hard not to smile.

She felt a little sorry for Ty. But she was glad for herself.

She didn't have the flu. *She* didn't have to go to bed. *She* was going to go watch TV. And *she* would have their parents all to herself tonight.

Ty stopped in the doorway.

He coughed.

He's coughing extra loud on

purpose, Sara thought. *Fake!*

"Could I please have some hot chocolate, Mom?" he asked. His voice was hoarse. "With whipped cream?"

Give me a break, thought Sara.

"Of course, dear," answered Mrs. Triceratops. "Sara will bring it up."

Sara's mouth dropped open.

"What?" she exclaimed. "Me? Why do I have to?"

"Because you're healthy," her mother replied. "And because I need to watch Tracy."

Sara pouted. Why should she be Ty's slave, just because she wasn't sick?

"I'll start the hot chocolate," Mrs. Triceratops continued. "Sara, could you bring me the thermometer from the medicine chest?"

Grumbling, Sara left the kitchen.

She passed the Christmas tree in the living room. For a second she forgot her bad mood, because the tree looked so beautiful.

There were strings of popcorn. Ornaments of all colors. Dino-sized candy canes on every branch, and brightly wrapped packages underneath.

On top was the best of all. A dainty pterodactyl angel. Its halo was gold. Its gown was white china sprayed with gold glitter.

She reached out to touch it.

She stumbled on something hard.

Tracy's blocks. "Oh, no!"

She lost her balance and staggered against the tree.

The angel tumbled down.

It landed on the brick floor near the fireplace and smashed into pieces.

The crash brought Sara's mother running.

"What happened?" she cried. Then she saw the mess.

16

She put her hands on her hips. "Honestly, Sara!"

In the kitchen Tracy was wailing. From upstairs Ty called, "Where's my hot chocolate?"

"As if I didn't have enough to worry about!" Mrs. Triceratops scolded.

Sara hung her head.

Her mother's voice grew softer. "I know, I know. It was an accident. It's okay. Look, Sara, just get me the thermometer. We'll sweep up the pieces later."

Sara ran off to the bathroom. She felt a big lump in her throat. She tried not to cry.

She studied herself in the mirror.

Her face was still bright green.

Her nose wasn't red.

Her eyes weren't watery.

At least she didn't have the flu. But she felt sick inside all the same.

Back in the kitchen, it was quiet.

Tracy was drinking a bottle of juice.

Mrs. Triceratops was stirring hot chocolate on the stove.

It smelled yummy. Sara's stomach growled.

Her mother put down her wooden spoon. She took the thermometer and gave Sara a hug. "You're such a big help, Sara."

Mrs. Triceratops poured some chocolate into a huge mug. She squirted whipped cream on top. She put the mug on a tray.

"Take this up to Ty. Then we'll have some ourselves."

"Don't you care if I get Ty's germs?"

Her mother smiled. "If you haven't gotten them yet, maybe you won't."

Sara took the tray upstairs. She turned away when she passed the

fireplace. She didn't want to see the broken angel.

She could hear Ty sneezing.

Suddenly she felt sorry for him.

Poor Ty, she thought. He might miss Cave City. And Christmas, too.

She opened his door.

All at once she didn't feel sorry anymore.

Ty looked too comfortable.

He was snuggled under a fluffy quilt. His eyes were closed. He had earphones on. A tape player was on the nightstand.

Comic books were scattered on the bed. They were his favorites: *Killer Iguanodons.*

Sara put the tray on the nightstand.

She looked at the tape player. Through the little window she could see the name of the tape.

"Albertasaurus and the Asteroids,"

she read out loud. "That's my brand-new tape!"

Ty's eyes flew open.

Sara yanked the tape out of the player.

"Hey!" he said weakly.

"I told you not to play that without my permission," she said.

"But I'm sick," protested Ty.

"Big deal," said Sara. "That doesn't mean you can do anything you want."

She stormed back downstairs.

Her mother had a mug of hot chocolate waiting for her.

Plain hot chocolate.

"Where's the whipped cream?" Sara asked.

"There was just a squirt left," Mrs. Triceratops answered. "It's all gone. I'm sorry."

Used it all on Ty's, thought Sara.

This was the worst day in the world!

CHAPTER
3

The night wasn't much better.

Ty and Tracy got all the attention. Sara got all the work.

Her mother cooked Ty's favorite spaghetti dinner. Then she sat with him while he ate.

Sara had to help with the dishes.

Her father brought a TV into Ty's bedroom. They watched a hockey game together.

Sara had to do her homework.

Mrs. Triceratops rocked Tracy. Mr. Triceratops read her a story about a baby dino's first Christmas.

Sara had to brush her teeth and put on her pajamas.

Sara's father went to check on Ty.

Her mother put Tracy to bed.

Then they both came back to the living room.

Finally! thought Sara. *My turn!*

"Can we make Christmas cookies now?" she asked her mother. "You promised."

Mrs. Triceratops was sitting with her feet propped up. "I know, Sara. But I'm so tired now. And it's late. Let's bake tomorrow."

Sara pouted. "You *promised!*"

Her father put down his *Dino Daily News.* "You should go to bed early, anyway," he told Sara. "With plenty of rest, maybe you won't get sick."

"I wish I *were* sick!" Sara shouted at them. "I hate being well!"

She ran upstairs.

In her bedroom mirror she looked closely at her face.

Still green.

Not a trace of sickly pink.

Sara sighed. She took the red Christmas bows off her horns. Carefully she hung them on the bedpost.

She crawled into bed. *Maybe tomorrow I'll get sick, too.*

When Sara got up the next morning she snuck into Ty's room. He was still asleep.

She placed her Albertasaurus and the Asteroids tape on the nightstand. She was sorry she had been mean about it the day before. After all, it wasn't Ty's fault he was sick and she wasn't.

She still wouldn't mind being sick, though. She tried to catch his germs.

She took big breaths through her mouth.

She rubbed her hands on his comic books.

It didn't work. She felt fine.

So she stomped through the snowdrifts to the bus. A freezing cold wind blew snow down her neck.

She thought of Ty, all nice and warm. She gritted her teeth.

The bus was only half full. Annette wasn't there. Some of Sara's other dino friends weren't there, either. But Maggie Megalosaurus was.

"Sit with me, Sara," Maggie called.

Sara plopped down next to Maggie. "I wish I were sick," she complained. "Even if it is almost Christmas. Sick people get all the attention."

"I'm glad I'm *not* sick," said Maggie. "Sick people lose their appetites."

Maggie loved to eat. She ate more than anyone else in Mrs. D.'s class.

Right now she was munching Santasaurus cookies. They had red colored sugar on them.

Sara noticed that the red was

coming off on Maggie's face and hands.

Maggie rolled her eyes. "I'd just die if I couldn't eat." She held out her bag of cookies. "Want one?"

Sara took off her mitten and grabbed a cookie.

Red color went onto her fingertips, too.

It made them sort of pink. Like the color Ty had looked yesterday.

Sara stared at her hand. She was getting an idea. A great idea! A great way to get some attention herself!

She ate the cookie in two bites.

She knew just what she would do right after school.

When Sara and Maggie got to Mrs. D.'s room, they saw lots of empty desks.

"Diana Deinonychus is absent," said Maggie. "So's Hank the Tank."

"No jokes today," said Sara sadly.

Hank Ankylosaur was the funniest dino in the third grade.

Patrick Apatosaurus was absent, too. Sara missed him already.

"School's going to be as boring as home," she said.

"More boring," said Spike. He was sharpening pencils on his spikes. "At least at home you can watch TV."

Sara frowned. "If your brother isn't hogging the set."

She couldn't wait to put her plan into action!

Mrs. D. came into the room. Six plaid wool mufflers were wound around her long neck.

"I'm not really sick," she told them. "But my throat hurts a little. I want to keep it warm today. And I won't be talking very much. Or very loudly."

Sara cheered up. Maybe Mrs. D. wouldn't give them a spelling test.

Spelling was Sara's worst subject.

"So please move up closer," her teacher said. "Sit in these empty desks up front. That way I won't have to shout your spelling words."

Sara sighed. This just wasn't her day.

Suddenly the wall calendar flapped. Paper chains on the bulletin boards rustled. A bow fell off the fish tank.

Something big was pounding down the hall.

"Here comes Rex," Spike said.

"Why couldn't *he* be sick?" Sara said.

"The germs probably refused to go near him," answered Spike.

Maggie and Sara laughed.

Mrs. D. frowned at them.

She tapped her tail.

Swish-thump. Swish-thump.

That meant she wanted quiet.

Rex burst into the classroom.

His lips were blue.

His boots were caked with snow.

"Rex," Mrs. D. said. "Late again?"

Rex was late almost every day.

"I had to walk!" he snarled. He glared at Spike. "Some stupid stegosaurus and his stupid friends messed up my bike. It's all scratched!"

"But even if it's scratched, can't you still ride it?" Mrs. D. asked.

Rex's eyes widened in horror. "Of course not! The scratches might rust in the snow. It needs a new paint job."

Rex marched to his desk. He leaned over to Spike.

"Anyone who messes with me and my bike better watch out! You're in big trouble, pointy-tail!"

Spike pushed back his shades. He grinned.

"Merry Christmas to you, too, Rex," he said.

Swish-thump.

"Time for our spelling test," Mrs. D. announced. "Let's get to work."

All the dinos took out pencils and paper.

"The first word is *faster*."

That one was easy.

"Festival."

That one was harder. Sara scratched her horns for a second. Then she wrote something down.

"Frosting."

"Yum!" said Maggie.

"Fossil," continued Mrs. D.

"Oh, phooey," Sara sighed. She could never remember that one.

After the spelling test Mrs. D. reminded them about permission slips for Cave City. "I have everyone's except yours, Rex. Aren't you going?"

The entire class turned to Rex. They had hopeful looks on their faces.

"Yeah," he grunted. "Yeah, I'm going."

Everyone groaned.

Swish-thump.

Rex smiled his nastiest smile at Spike. "It will be a lot of *fun*. I can hardly wait."

Spike didn't say anything. But Sara was scared. Was Rex planning something super-special mean? She'd better tell Ty when she got home.

At ten o'clock the dinos went to gym.

Ms. Iguanodon was the gym teacher. "Jump ropes today!" she called.

Usually Sara loved jumping rope. But that was when Annette was there. They always counted how many times they could jump in a minute.

"I miss Annette," Sara told Maggie. "I mean, I'm glad *you're* here. But still, I miss her."

31

"I understand," said Maggie. She was hiding behind a stack of tumbling mats, sneaking more cookies.

Suddenly she stopped eating. "Have a cookie," she told Sara. "In fact, have them all."

Sara was amazed. Maggie, giving away all her cookies?

"Don't you want any more?" she asked.

"I—I don't feel—AH-CHOO!"

Maggie walked slowly up to Ms. Iguanodon. Her tail was dragging.

"Another one bites the dust," observed Spike.

Suddenly a rope smacked him on the foot.

"Jump! Jump!" Rex was yelling. His rope was bunched up like a whip.

He lashed out again.

This time Spike caught the rope with his tail. Expertly he twirled his tail,

winding the rope around it tightly.

Rex was pulled along with the rope. He toppled over with a crash.

Spike unwound his end and let the rope fall.

Rex slowly got up. "Now you're in *deep* trouble, Stegosaurus," he growled. "You're history!"

Rex looked madder than Sara could ever remember. She and Spike backed away.

"He's really mad this time," she said. "You'd better watch out. We'd *all* better watch out."

Spike just shrugged. "I'm not afraid of Rex," he said.

After lunch Mrs. D.'s class and Mr. Pterodactyl's class sang Christmas carols together. Between carols Mr. Pterodactyl told Christmas jokes.

"What did Santasaurus say when he planted his garden? Hoe, hoe, hoe!"

Mr. Pterodactyl loved his corny jokes. Sara liked them, too. But it made her sad to look at him. He reminded her of the pterodactyl angel she'd broken.

Then she cheered up. After all, he looked like Tory Pterodactyl, too. In just a couple of days Sara would be in Cave City, watching her and the Ice Screams.

Before that, though, she had her own special plan to follow.

Before that, she was going to get some attention.

And it would be about time!

CHAPTER
4

Ty was in the kitchen when Sara got home. He was wearing his Killer Iguanodons bathrobe. Comic books lay on the counter in front of him.

He was digging into a heaping bowl of Dino-Mint ice cream.

Mrs. Triceratops had stayed home from work. She was sitting next to Ty, making a shopping list.

Sara frowned. "Why is *he* out of bed?"

"He's really much better," Mrs. Triceratops told her. "But he still needs a little TLC."

"What's TLC?" asked Sara.

"Tender loving care," her mother explained.

I want some too, Sara thought. *I want lots and lots of TLC.*

"Hi, hi, hi, hi," called Tracy from her high chair. She banged on the tray with a spoon.

"Tracy's better, too," her mother said. "Soon we'll all be back to normal."

Not before I get my turn, thought Sara.

"I want ice cream, too," she said.

Ty shook his head. His mouth was full. "Uh-uh. Uhmor."

Sara was furious. "What? No more?"

She yanked open the freezer. Sure enough. No ice cream. She spotted the empty container in the trash can.

"Thanks a lot, Ty!" she yelled.

Tracy gave a startled little cry.

"Shh, Sara. We'll get more. It's on my list." Her mother's voice was understanding. "Have a bunch of bananas."

"I don't want bananas," Sara muttered. "I want ice cream."

She slammed the freezer shut. Her face was angry.

"Well, at least can we make Christmas cookies now?" she demanded.

Mrs. Triceratops smothered a sigh. "Sure we can. You take out the ingredients while I finish this list."

Sara opened the refrigerator. She took out eggs, milk, and butter.

She opened a cupboard. She took out flour, sugar, salt, and spices.

From another shelf she took a box with little bottles inside. Dino-Dye, the box said.

Each bottle held a different food coloring. There were red, blue, yellow, and green.

Ty was reading his comic books again. Mrs. Triceratops' head was bent

38

over her list. Little Tracy was busy with her bottle.

No one was watching Sara.

Quickly she slid the bottle of red Dino-Dye into her pocket.

"All set, Mom," she said.

Sara and her mother baked green wreath cookies. They baked white snowflake cookies with coconut. They baked ginger cookies.

The kitchen smelled Christmasy and sweet.

"Now we should make some Santasauruses," said her mother. She reached inside the Dino-Dye box.

There was no red.

"That's funny," she said. "I was sure that box had all the colors." She shrugged. "Oh, well. Our Santasauruses will have blue suits. Or yellow ones."

"That will be pretty," Sara agreed.

When the Santasauruses were done, Sara hung up her apron. "I'd better go do my homework," she said.

Mrs. Triceratops looked surprised. "What a good girl! Okay. I'm going to make something special for dinner. To celebrate everyone feeling better."

Almost everyone, thought Sara.

Upstairs she pulled a stack of tissues out of a box. Then she poured red Dino-Dye on them. She watched as the red soaked in.

Then she rubbed her face with the wet tissues.

In a minute she looked in her bedroom mirror.

"It worked!" she cried.

She looked awful. Pink and sickly.

Sara laughed out loud. Then she flopped on her bed with her arms behind her head.

She thought of all the attention she

would finally be getting.

Her favorite foods.

Everybody waiting on her.

Everybody worried about her.

It was going to be great!

It wasn't too long before Mrs. Triceratops called, "Dinner!"

Sara walked slowly into the kitchen. She made her tail droop. She lowered her head.

A delicious smell drifted toward her.

Pizzas! Four homemade pizzas!

Each one was as big as a baby dino's wading pool.

Each one was covered with bubbly melted cheese.

Sara's mouth was watering.

Mrs. Triceratops smiled at her. Then the smile froze. "What happened to you?"

"Let me take a look," said her father.

"What a dreadful pink color," her

mother said. "But you were nice and green a little while ago."

"Sometimes these things come up suddenly," her father said. He peered closely at Sara's face. "*Very* suddenly."

Her mother looked at her, too.

Then her parents looked at each other. She saw her father wink at her mother.

What's he doing? Sara wondered. *Why don't they hurry up and start the TLC?*

"You'd better go up to bed, young lady," her mother said.

Sara looked at the pizza. It was still steaming and bubbling.

Ty was loading slices of it onto his plate. Tracy had messy fistfuls of it in her hands.

"Maybe I could eat some pizza first," Sara said weakly. "Just a tiny bite."

"That wouldn't be a good idea," her

43

father said firmly. "It's too spicy. It might upset your stomach."

"Go on up to bed," her mother said. "I'll bring up some toast and tea in a little while."

Toast and tea! This wasn't what she had planned!

Ty folded a slice of pizza and crammed it into his mouth. He grinned at her around it.

His lips moved. *Fake,* he mouthed.

Sara ignored him. She made her voice even weaker. "No hot chocolate?"

"It's all gone," Mrs. Triceratops said.

Sara went slowly upstairs.

She threw herself on the bed.

Some plan this was turning out to be!

It seemed as if she waited for hours. Didn't anyone care about her at all?

Finally her mother carried in a tray.

Sara could see a steaming mug and a plate with two brown slabs.

Sara wrinkled her nose.

She coughed as hard as she could. "Can I have the TV in my room?"

Her mother shook her head. "I don't think so, dear. You should sleep."

She patted Sara's horns and left.

Sara nibbled at the toast. It was as dry as an old sponge. Yuck.

In a minute the door opened.

It was Ty. He was still in his Killer Iguanodons bathrobe.

"You're faking," he said. "Phony baloney."

"Go away," said Sara. She coughed a lot of times.

Ty just laughed.

"It's no fun being sick," he said.

Sara hated to admit it. But so far, Ty was right.

CHAPTER
5

Sunlight streamed in through the curtains.

Sara threw back the covers.

Then she remembered.

She was pretending to be sick.

She flopped back on her pillows.

Today maybe she'd finally get some attention.

Then she remembered something else. "Uh-oh," she muttered.

She jumped out of bed and ran to the mirror.

The sick pink color was fading. Healthy green was showing through.

Quickly Sara soaked tissues with Dino-Dye. She rubbed them on her face. Then she leaped back into bed.

Just in time. Her mother was coming

into the room. But why was she wearing her coat?

"How are you feeling?" asked Mrs. Triceratops.

Sara coughed. "Not too good," she said weakly. "Why do you have your coat on?"

"Because I'm going to work," her mother explained. "I can't miss two days in a row. And now that Tracy and Ty are better..."

"But what about me?" Sara cried.

"Mrs. Saurolophus will stay with you."

"That old fossil?"

"Sara, that's not nice."

"Well, she's about two hundred years old. She never lets us do anything when she baby-sits."

Her mother sat on the bed. She held Sara's hand. "You're sick," she said. "Remember? You won't want to do anything today except rest."

Sara frowned. She flounced back on her pillows.

Her mother kissed her forehead. "Bye, dear. I'll bring home some hot chocolate mix tonight."

But I want some now, Sara thought angrily.

She punched her pillows.

A whole day with Mrs. Saurolophus. And no hot chocolate.

A fat tear rolled down Sara's nose. It made a pink splat on the pillowcase.

Quickly she turned over the pillow.

I can't even cry, she thought. How had she come up with this stupid plan?

The day dragged by.

First she picked up a mystery book. Mystery books were her favorite. But she couldn't get interested today.

Then she nibbled at the toast and oatmeal Mrs. Saurolophus brought her.

They tasted as yucky as they looked.

She rewrote her Christmas list:

> *Bows for horns*
> *Clothes for Barbiesaurus dolls*
> *Pierced horn-rings*

Mom and Dad thought she was too young to have her horns pierced. But maybe they'd change their minds.

She kept writing:

> *Mystery books*
> *New ice skates*

That made her think of the trip to Cave City tomorrow. She'd better get her healthy green color back!

She ran into the bathroom and scrubbed her face hard. Most of the red came off. She hid the washcloth at the bottom of the hamper.

Sara wandered back into her bedroom. Now she was all set for Cave City.

She wondered again if Rex would

try something really mean there.

We'll all be extra careful, she thought.

Soon Sara dozed off. When she woke up the sun was almost gone.

Mrs. Saurolophus was leaning over her. "How are you, dear?"

"Fine," Sara tried to say. But it wouldn't come out.

What came out instead was, "Ah-choo!"

Her throat was scratchy. She felt as if she'd swallowed an apatosaurus's mitten.

Her horns were throbbing.

She was freezing cold.

Mrs. Saurolophus put another quilt on her. "Take these," she said, handing Sara a glass of water and two pills.

The pills felt as big as volleyballs in Sara's throat.

She was really sick!

Now, when she didn't want to be!

Now, when the trip to Cave City was tomorrow!

"I'll get better fast," she promised herself. But she was too sleepy to try.

When she awoke it was nighttime. Ty was standing by her bed.

He actually looked sorry for her.

He was holding a tray. It had a big mug of hot chocolate on it. With a huge gob of whipped cream.

She didn't even want it.

"No, thanks," she whispered.

"No phony baloney anymore," he said. "Right?"

"Right," she croaked.

"Don't worry. Maybe you'll be better tomorrow."

Sara nodded. But all she could say was, "Ah-choo!"

The next morning Sara did feel a bit better. Everything ached a little less.

But her nose still felt like a water balloon. And she couldn't stop sneezing and coughing.

"I'm sorry, dear," said her mother. "Daddy and I will take you to Cave City next week during vacation."

"It won't be the same," said Sara. The big lump was back in her throat.

"I know," said her mother. "But it will be fun anyway. You'll see."

Ty stopped in. He was carrying his ice skates.

"I'm sorry you can't go," he told her. "Really."

"Me, too," said Sara. Her lip started to quiver.

She made it stop.

Then she remembered something. "Watch out for Rex," she told her brother. "He might do something really mean. *Really* m—Ah—Ah—choo!"

"We'll be careful," Ty promised.

CHAPTER
6

Sara settled herself in a chair near the Christmas tree. Mrs. Saurolophus said she could. She was bored with being in bed.

An icebag was on her aching head.

A box of tissues was next to her.

She blew her nose. HONK!

The top of the Christmas tree looked empty. Her parents had promised to buy a new angel. But Sara missed the old one.

She sighed and leaned back.

She wondered what her friends were doing right now. . . .

While Sara was sitting by the tree, her friends were sitting on a bus. They were waiting to go to Cave City.

Ty sat with Hank the Tank.

Spike and Patrick sat behind them.

Annette and Diana sat across the aisle.

Maggie was still sick, like Sara.

"Do you know how the Ice Screams are going to dress up today?" Diana asked.

The Ice Screams picked a different Christmas theme every year. They wore costumes to match.

Last year they were Rudolph and the Rein-Dinos.

"I don't know," said Annette. She looked around the bus. "But I do know something else."

"What's that?" asked Spike.

Annette's grin looked a mile wide. "Rex isn't here!"

Hank turned his face up. He pretended to be gazing at the sky.

"Thank you, Santasaurus, for this wonderful Christmas present."

"Maybe Rex is sick," said Diana hopefully.

"*Maybe?*" said Hank. "Of *course* he's sick. He's the sickest dino around."

"I meant with the flu," said Diana.

"Well, *I'm* really happy he's not here," Ty told Spike. "And you should be, too. Sara was worried he would try to get us back for the snowball fight. You know, for hitting him and his bike. And for what you did in gym yesterday. She told me all about it."

"Nothing scares Spike," Patrick said proudly. Spike was his best friend.

The bus doors closed.

There was a loud pounding. "Open up!"

The doors opened again.

Rex hurled himself aboard.

Everyone groaned.

56

Swish-thump.

Mrs. D. was frowning at them. "Let's not forget the holiday spirit," she said.

Rex thumped up the aisle.

He wore his usual clothes. Black ski jacket. Black boots. Black gloves.

"Rex looks so Christmas-y and cheerful," Hank whispered.

Mrs. D. wasn't watching anymore.

Rex rapped Hank on the head with his fist.

Then he grabbed Patrick's hat. He held it just out of Patrick's reach.

"Let me have that!" Patrick cried.

"Give it back to him, man," demanded Spike.

"Gonna make me?" sneered Rex.

From behind him Annette grabbed the hat. She tossed it to Patrick.

Rex made a fist at her.

He turned to Spike. "See you on the ice, needle-tail."

He turned to Ty. "Hope you have a good *trip,* horn-face!"

"I wonder what he meant by that," said Hank.

"Oh, who cares," Annette said.

Soon they arrived at Cave City and scrambled out of the bus.

The rink was huge.

At one end was a gigantic Christmas tree. At the other end was a place to put on skates and buy snacks.

In between were dinos in sweaters and scarves, skating happily.

"Now stay together," said Mrs. D. "I'll be watching from over there." She pointed at a row of seats.

The dinos laced on their skates and got on the ice.

Diana was the best skater. She could skate backwards. She could spin around without falling.

Annette was the fastest. She kept

challenging everyone to races. She always won.

Spike was the coolest skater. He glided and skimmed. He used the spikes on his tail as brakes.

After skating for about an hour, the dinos stopped for hot chocolate.

"I don't see Rex cutting any fancy figure 8's," said Hank.

"He's over there," said Ty. "He's not skating."

Rex was slouched over near the Christmas tree.

"Why did he come if he's not going to skate?" Patrick asked.

"He knew we'd be heartbroken without him," said Hank.

Just then skaters dressed up as Santasauruses started gliding through the crowd. They handed out popcorn balls wrapped in red and green cellophane. They carried the popcorn balls in great big sacks.

"Move to the sidelines," they called out. "Time for the show!"

The dinos heard flapping overhead. They looked up and gasped. Five beautiful angels were flying above them!

The angels flew in a V. Now the dinos could see their gold-bladed skates.

They flew lower. The one at the point of the V dipped a wing.

It was Tory Pterodactyl.

Everyone cheered and whistled.

"Wow!" said Ty.

"She's even prettier than on TV!" said Patrick.

The Ice Screams swooped down. They skimmed across the ice.

Tory *was* gorgeous. She had a gold halo. She wore a white gown with gold glitter on it.

The other Ice Screams wore blue.

Gracefully they took their places.

Then they started to dance a Christmas ballet. It was called the Beak-Cracker.

Ty was enjoying the show. It was great to feel well again!

His eyes wandered across the rink.

Something was wrong.

Something was missing.

Something big and mean and nasty.

"Rex," he said to himself.

He looked all around.

Rex had disappeared.

Ty's heart started pounding.

He nudged Spike. "Rex is gone!"

Spike shrugged. "So? Good!"

"Maybe he's getting ready to get back at us!"

"Oh, relax, man," Spike said.

The Ice Screams finished the ballet. They started doing tricks.

They did cartwheels and flips. They made a pyramid with Tory on top.

For their last number the Ice

Screams skated to the middle of the rink. Then each one skated off alone.

They skated hard and fast. Chips of ice flashed off their skates.

Then they moved aside.

There were two words carved in the ice.

HAPPY HOLIDAYS!!

The dinos went wild. What a show!

Now the Santasauruses were moving through the crowd again. "Free-style skating," they called. "Special prize for the best routine."

Patrick stopped one of them. "Any more popcorn balls?"

"All gone," said the Santasaurus. "A whole sack of them disappeared."

"That's funny," said Hank. "Maybe Maggie *is* here after all."

The dinos swarmed onto the ice.

Maybe I can win the prize, Ty thought.

"Let's make a whip!" yelled Annette.

All the dinos linked arms.

Spike was on the inside end.

Ty was on the end near the sidelines.

The ice was crowded with dinos. The seats around the rink were packed.

Ty could pick out Mrs. D. by her long neck. She was waving at them.

Suddenly he noticed something on the sidelines. It was a big Santasaurus sack. It looked full.

Something moved behind the sack.

Ty saw a black-jacketed arm reached inside. A black-gloved hand pulled out some popcorn balls.

"Watch out, guys!" he yelled to the others. "Look! Rex is getting ready to attack us with popcorn balls."

He pointed frantically toward the sack on the sidelines.

Just then a wave of red and green popcorn balls came spilling across the ice. They were rolling right up ahead of the dinos.

"Hey, needle-tail!" a mean voice shouted. "Hey, horn-face! See you next *fall!*"

"Separate!" yelled Ty.

Immediately they moved apart.

Diana spun away from the rolling popcorn balls.

Annette leaped over them.

Patrick slid through them on his stomach. He made a path for Spike and Hank and Ty. Spike and Hank let go of Ty and skated off to the side.

Ty spun around and around in fancy circles.

Everyone else had stopped skating. Everyone else was clapping for Ty.

Tory Pterodactyl herself came gliding over.

"Great skating!" she told Ty. "You win the prize."

Tory handed Ty a box covered with gold paper.

Carefully he unwrapped it.

All the dinos crowded around to see. Patrick hung his long neck over Ty's shoulder.

It was a china pterodactyl angel. It had a gold halo. Its gown was white with gold glitter.

Ty gasped. "It looks just like the one we used to have on our tree! Sara broke it by accident."

There was gold writing on the angel's gown.

"Merry Christmas to a special dino," read Patrick. "Love, Tory Pterodactyl."

Ty grinned. "I have a great idea."

He explained his plan to the others.

Mrs. D. joined them. When she heard Ty's plan, she had an idea, too.

"Time to go, everyone," she called.

It was getting late. The crowd at the

66

rink had thinned out. Everyone was heading for home.

Almost everyone.

A certain tyrannosaurus had to stay late.

First he had to pick up all the popcorn balls from the ice.

Then he had to pick up every piece of trash and litter in the whole rink.

A smiling Santasaurus watched Rex work.

The Santasaurus waved to Mrs. D. and her dinos as they left.

"Ho, ho, ho!" he shouted.

"Ha, ha, ha!" they shouted back.

CHAPTER
7

At the Triceratops house it was almost time for dinner.

Sara felt much better. Her nose wasn't running anymore. She hadn't sneezed in an hour.

She wished Ty would hurry.

He should have been home by now. She wanted to know what had happened at Cave City.

Mrs. Triceratops came into the living room. "I'm making macaroni and cheese," she said. "With that dino macaroni you like so much. And we have gallons of hot chocolate and whipped cream. Want anything else?"

"No, thanks," Sara answered.

Then the words just burst out of her.

"Why do you have all my favorite things *now?* Why wasn't anyone nice to me yesterday?"

Mrs. Triceratops put her arm around Sara. "Because today you're really sick."

Sara's eyes widened. "But how did you know I wasn't sick yesterday?"

"Parents have a way of knowing these things," Mrs. Triceratops said with a wink.

Sara's chin dropped down to her chest.

"I just wanted some TLC."

Her mother hugged her harder. "I know you did, Sara. But you know you don't have to pretend to be sick just to get some attention."

Sara sighed and leaned back. "Well, it seemed that way the other day. I'm sorry, Mom. I won't do it again." She blew her nose. "I wish Ty would

69

come home. He's really late."

"I'm sure he'll be here soon," her mother said, kissing her on the top of her head.

Just then the front door opened. A blast of cold air came into the snug room.

"Ho, ho, ho," a cheery voice called.

Sara could hear jingle bells.

"We wish you a Merry Christmas," voices sang.

Sara couldn't believe her eyes. Practically all her friends from Dino School were in the living room.

Patrick and Hank.

Spike.

Annette and Diana.

And, of course, Ty.

The dinos had jingle bells attached to their horns and tails. They shook and jingled happily.

Ty was holding a pretty gold box.

Sara clapped her hands. What fun!

But who was that with them?

Someone tall.

Carrying a big sack.

Wearing a red suit and a red stocking cap.

And a long, long white beard.

"Santasaurus!" Sara cried.

The figure bent down. "Ho, ho, ho. I've heard there's a very special dino in this house."

Mrs. Triceratops hugged Sara again. "She's very, *very* special to us."

Sara started to giggle, but it turned into a sneeze.

"AH-CHOO!"

The other dinos leaped away.

So did the Santasaurus.

"Sorry," Sara apologized. "How was Cave City?"

"Great," said Ty. "At least, as great as it could be without you."

He held out the box. "Here."

"Ty won it," said Spike.

"Everyone helped," said Ty.

"And we all wanted you to have it," said Santasaurus.

"For me?" Sara asked. She was so surprised.

She opened the box. "Oh!" she gasped. "Oh!"

It was the most beautiful pterodactyl angel she had ever seen. It was even prettier than the one she had broken.

And even more special. Because this was a present from her friends. And her brother.

She read the writing on it out loud. "Merry Christmas to a special dino."

"That's you, Sara," said Patrick shyly.

Mrs. Triceratops took the angel. Gently she placed it on top of the tree. She stood back to admire it. "It looks

72

as though it belongs there."

"It *does* belong there," said Sara. "It's perfect. How did you win it?"

Her friends told her about what had happened at Cave City.

"Mrs. D. made Rex pick up all the popcorn balls he had thrown," said Diana.

"And he had to pick up all the rest of the trash at the rink, too," said Annette.

"And after Christmas vacation he's going to be wiping a lot of chalkboards at Dino School," finished Santasaurus.

Sara smiled at the tall figure. "How do *you* know?"

Santasaurus grinned back. Then the long, long beard was pulled off. Underneath was a long, long neck with four mufflers on it.

It was Mrs. D.

"I knew it!" said Sara.

"We stopped at school for the costume," the teacher said. "I've been saving it for a very special occasion."

She looked fondly at all her students. "And this is definitely special!"

She reached into her sack. "Popcorn ball, anyone? Then we have to go."

"We're bringing the rest of the popcorn balls to Maggie," Hank explained.

Sara was so happy.

She wanted to thank her teacher.

She wanted to thank her friends.

She wanted to thank her brother.

She opened her mouth to speak.

But all that came out was, "AH-CHOO!"